Ruford
Visits the Farm

written & illustrated by
Susan Lienau

Print ISBN: 978-1-7323526-2-9

Published and printed in the United States of America by the Write Place, Inc. For more information, please contact:

the Write Place, Inc.
809 W. 8th Street, Suite 2
Pella, Iowa 50219
www.thewriteplace.biz

Cover and interior design by Alexis Thomas, the Write Place, Inc.
Illustrations by Susan Lienau.

Copies of this book may be ordered online at Amazon and BarnesandNoble.com.

View other Write Place titles at www.thewriteplace.biz.

This book is dedicated to my four sons, Nile, Noah, Isaiah, and Ian; my three grandsons, Raymond, Earl, and Ren; and my many nephews, nieces, great-nephews, and great-nieces.

To all of you, I would like this book to be a reminder to always pursue your passions in life, no matter how old you grow.

I would like to thank my husband, Ronald, for encouraging me to follow my dream of being creative and exploring my talents. A special thank-you goes to my niece, Glenna Meyer-Munuswamy, for helping with the editing of this story and believing in this project from the start.

I love you all.

Where Did Ruford Fly?

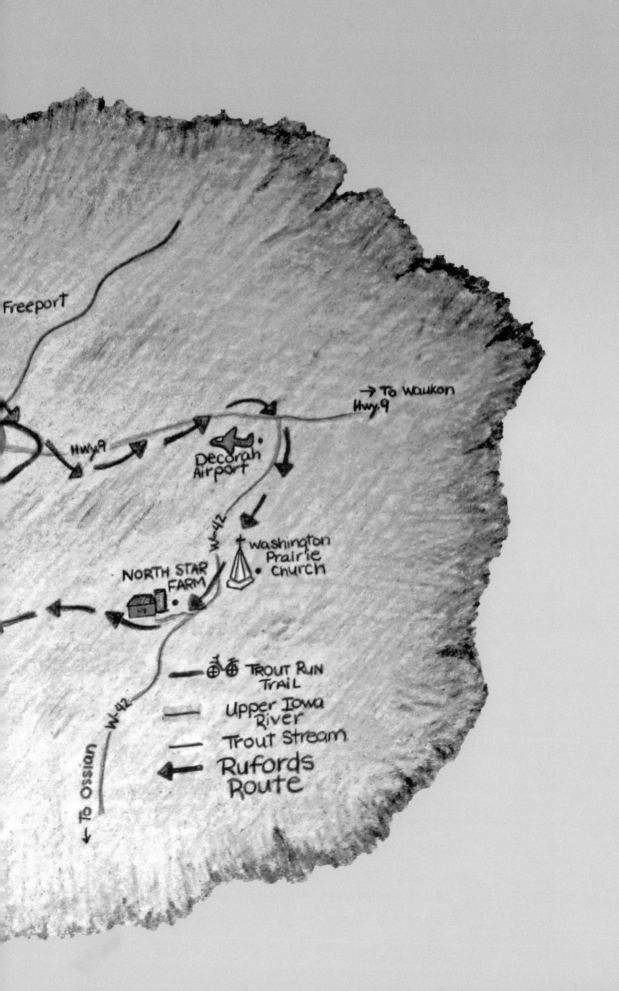

Freeport

→ To Waukon
Hwy 9

Hwy 9

Decorah
Airport

W-42

Washington
Prairie
church

NORTH STAR
FARM

🚲🚲 Trout Run
Trail

Upper Iowa
River

Trout Stream

Rufords
Route

W-42

To Ossian

When Ruford the Eagle woke up in his family's
warm nest in Northeast Iowa, he was very excited.
It was a beautiful morning, and Mama and Papa
Eagle were sending him on his first solo flight.

"Today is my very BIG day," he said as he prepared
to take off. "I am ready to explore!"

Up so high in the air, Ruford could see everything—from the fish hatchery to Trout Run Trail and the beautiful bluffs. The Upper Iowa River was flowing through Decorah, the prettiest little town in Iowa.

"What is that over there?" Ruford asked, spying something strange. "It looks like a very large bird, but it's shiny!"

Ruford soared toward the strange-looking bird and called out, "Hi, I'm Ruford! What's your name?"

The bird did not answer.

Ruford was puzzled by this bird. It had wings, but no feathers. It had a nose, but no beak.

"What kind of bird are you?" Ruford asked. Still, the bird did not answer. He would have to ask Papa Eagle about it when he got home.

Suddenly, Ruford's stomach grumbled.

"It's time for me to find something to eat," he declared. Away he flew to look for a snack.

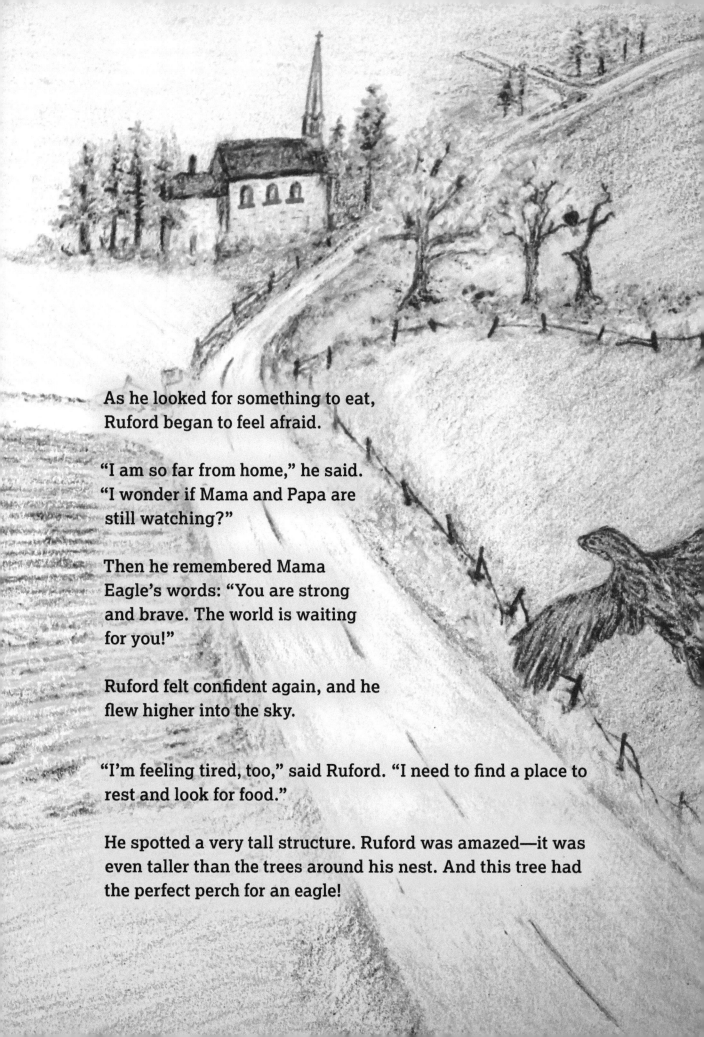

As he looked for something to eat,
Ruford began to feel afraid.

"I am so far from home," he said.
"I wonder if Mama and Papa are
still watching?"

Then he remembered Mama
Eagle's words: "You are strong
and brave. The world is waiting
for you!"

Ruford felt confident again, and he
flew higher into the sky.

"I'm feeling tired, too," said Ruford. "I need to find a place to
rest and look for food."

He spotted a very tall structure. Ruford was amazed—it was
even taller than the trees around his nest. And this tree had
the perfect perch for an eagle!

Ruford landed but was again puzzled. This tree was tall and sturdy, but it had no leaves, or branches, or nests!

"What a strange and glorious tree," he cried. "Wait until I tell Mama and Papa about this!"

Ruford's stomach grumbled. "Uh oh, I better find some food soon."

He took off again and began looking at the fields below for his next meal.

Something caught his eye...a big red building down in the valley. He saw strange animals moving around it. Ignoring his hunger, Ruford flew toward them.

"Maybe those animals have food to share..."

Ruford landed on the fence next to the red building and spotted a cow.

"Hi, I'm Ruford."

"Good morning," said the cow. "My name is Gem. What brings you to North Star Farm?"

"This is my first solo flight," replied Ruford. "I've never been to a farm before. And I've never met a cow."

"And I've never met a bird like you!" said Gem the Cow. "What kind of bird are you?"

"I am an eagle," said Ruford. "You probably did not recognize me, since my head and tail feathers won't be white until I am five years old."

"Oh, I was born with my white spots," said Gem.
"Where do you live?"

"Near the fish hatchery—in a great, big nest," answered Ruford.

"A nest? Do your friends live there, too?"

"No. It's just Mama, Papa, and me."

"Well, come meet some of my friends," said Gem.
"There are so many animals on the farm!"

"Good morning, Paisley," called Gem.
"Meet my new friend, Ruford."

"Hello, Ruford," said Paisley the Pig.
"What brings you to North Star Farm?"

"I'm out exploring," said Ruford.

Paisley squealed with delight. "I love
exploring, too!"

"Have you met the rest of the animals?" asked Paisley.

"No. Just you and Gem," replied Ruford.

"Let's go! You must meet Gretta," Paisley said excitedly.

Just then, a little farm pony came trotting up.

"Who do you have there, Gem?" asked Gretta the Pony.

"This is our new friend, Ruford. He is here on his first solo flight."

Ruford noticed the bright pink halter Gretta was wearing.

"What is that pink thing on your face?" he asked.

"Oh, that's my halter," said Gretta. "Farmer Randy ties a rope to it when he leads me around the farm. It would be fun to be free like you!"

"Have you seen Cindy?" asked Gem.

"Not since breakfast," Gretta answered. "Let's go find her."

Oh, breakfast, thought Ruford. *I sure would like a bite to eat!* He had not even seen a mouse this morning.

"Cindy! Where are you?" whinnied Gretta. "We have company!"

Just then, a dog came sprinting around the house. It let out two loud barks and was running right toward Ruford. Ruford was scared. He was just about to take flight when Gem stepped in.

Gem scolded Cindy. "That is no way to treat a guest! This is our new friend, Ruford."

"Sorry," apologized Cindy the Dog. "I just get so excited when we have visitors! Can we still be friends?"

"Of course," said Ruford.

"Do you want to go to the backyard and dig for bones?" Cindy asked.

Paisley and Gretta also wanted to play with their new friend.

"Ruford doesn't want to dig for bones, Cindy. He wants to go for a run in the pasture with me," said Gretta.

"But I want to take him for a roll in the mud!" cried Paisley.

"Remember, you three. Ruford has more friends to meet," said Gem. "Besides, I'm sure Ruford's wings could use a rest."

"All right," grunted Paisley. "Should we go find Whiskers?"

"I last saw Whiskers sleeping in the barn," said Cindy. "I promised I wouldn't chase her because she said she was too tired this morning."

So Ruford the Eagle, Gem the Cow, Paisley the Pig, Gretta the Horse, and Cindy the Dog headed toward the barn to find Whiskers.

In the barn, Whiskers the Cat was curled up on a pile of hay.

"Wake up, Whiskers. Meet our new friend, Ruford," said Gem, as she nudged the cat with her nose.

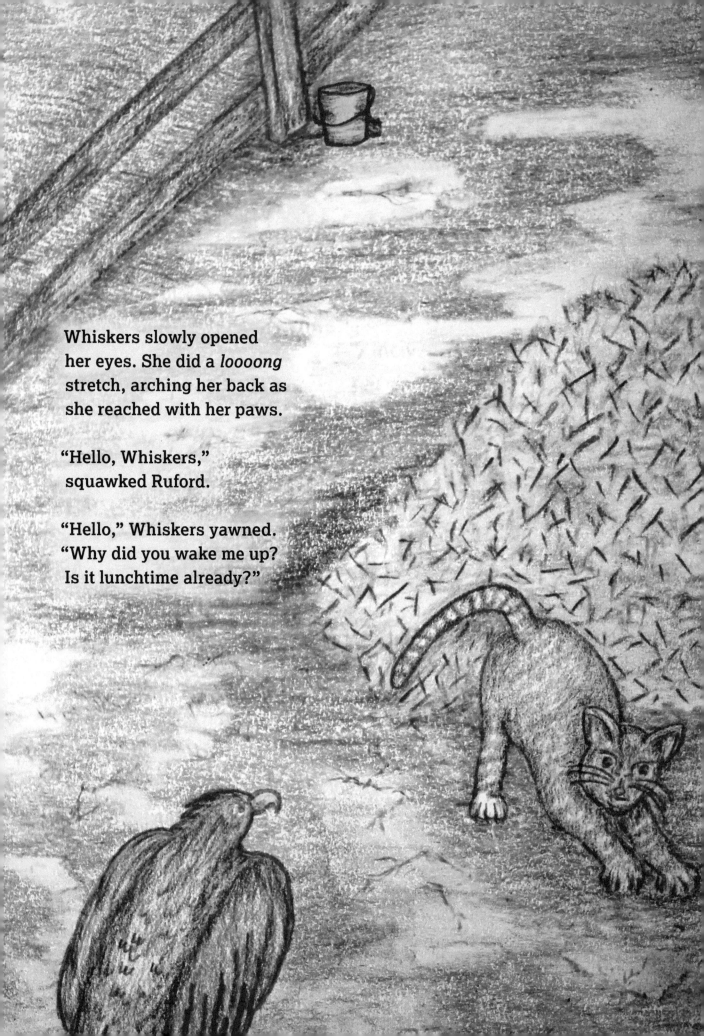

Whiskers slowly opened her eyes. She did a *loooong* stretch, arching her back as she reached with her paws.

"Hello, Whiskers," squawked Ruford.

"Hello," Whiskers yawned. "Why did you wake me up? Is it lunchtime already?"

Ruford's stomach let out a growl.

"I'm sorry," said Ruford. "I was so excited this morning that I forgot to eat breakfast. I'm so hungry I could eat a whole mouse. Are there any mice on the farm?"

Ruford's new friends were shocked.

Whiskers hissed, Gretta neighed, Gem mooed, Paisley grunted, and Cindy let out a whimper.

"We do have a mouse here, but you can't eat him," explained Whiskers.

"We are all friends at North Star Farm," whinnied Gretta. "Farmer Randy hand-picked each one of us to live together, including Eddie the Field Mouse."

"Eddie should be around here somewhere, but he is awfully good at hiding," said Cindy.

Ruford felt embarrassed. He didn't know a mouse could be your friend!

"I'm sorry," Ruford apologized. "I would never eat one of your friends. Do you think Eddie the Field Mouse will still meet me?"

"If we trust you, then Eddie will trust you," said Whiskers. "Eddie? Will you come out from wherever you are hiding and meet Ruford?"

Eddie squeaked in fear.

"There is no need to be scared, Eddie. We have all met Ruford, and he won't hurt you," coaxed Gem.

Eddie peeked around the corner from where he had been hiding since Ruford first landed on the farm.

"Hi," said Eddie, still not sure that he could trust an eagle.

"It is nice to meet you," replied Ruford, trying not to scare the little mouse.

Hearing Ruford speak made Eddie feel comfortable, and he was no longer scared.

The new bunch of friends made their way outside. Just then, they heard the creak of a screen door opening. They lifted their heads to look at the house and saw Farmer Randy walking toward the barn. He wore overalls and a hat and had a friendly face.

"Good morning, everybody! I see we have someone new," said Farmer Randy.

"This is our new friend, Ruford," explained Gem. "He is on his first solo flight, all the way from the fish hatchery."

"I saw your beautiful red barn and stopped to meet all the animals," said Ruford.

"We love visitors at North Star Farm," said Randy. "I hope you've made some new friends."

"Yes, sir! Everybody has been so nice. This sure is a fun place to be."

"We are one big family here on the farm. We spend our days taking care of the land and enjoying the sunshine," explained Farmer Randy.

"It would be so fun to be part of your family," said Ruford.

Randy replied, "Each one of these animals has a special place in my heart. And now you do, too. Any time you want to stop at North Star Farm, you can be part of our family."

"Really?! You mean it?!" exclaimed Ruford. "I can't wait to tell Mama and Papa all about you!"

"I've had such a wonderful time meeting all of you, but I should get home so Mama and Papa don't get worried," said Ruford.

"Have a safe flight, Ruford," said Farmer Randy.

Ruford took off, then circled over the farm, saying goodbye to all his new friends.

"Goodbye, Gem. Goodbye, Paisley. Goodbye, Gretta and Cindy. Goodbye, Whiskers and Eddie. Goodbye, Farmer Randy."

"Goodbye, Ruford!" they all called.

Ruford flew the long journey home. When he reached the fish hatchery, he could see Mama and Papa in the distance, waiting for him in their nest. Ruford's tummy let out a loud rumble, reminding him of his hunger. He looked down at all the trout swimming in the tanks.

The hatchery won't miss just one fish, he thought.

Ruford swooped down, grabbed
a trout with his large talons,
and flew to his nest
so he could finally eat.

Mama and Papa were happy to see him return.

"You must have had a big day," said Papa Eagle.

"I sure did," cried Ruford as he ate his trout. "I met
so many new friends! I wish you could have
been there with me."

"I wish we could have, too," said Papa Eagle,
as he winked at Mama.

1. How many times can you find Ruford's papa in the book? (Look closely!)

2. How many orange butterflies do you see in the book?

3. How many cars do you see in the book?

4. How many airplanes are at the airport?

5. What color is Gretta's halter?

6. How many times can you find Eddie?

7. What does Farmer Randy have in his pocket?

CPSIA information can be obtained
at www.ICGtesting.com
Printed in the USA
LVHW072342311018
595555LV00004B/8/P

* 9 7 8 1 7 3 2 3 5 2 6 2 9 *